CARROTS ARE NOT

Ooopsie!

FOR PARROTS

by Merri López

Balboa Press books may be ordered through booksellers or by contacting:

Balboa Press
A Division of Hay House
1663 Liberty Drive
Bloomington, IN 47403
www.balboapress.com
1 (877) 407-4847

ISBN: 978-1-9822-2234-5 (sc)
ISBN: 978-1-9822-2233-8 (e)
Library of Congress Control Number: 2019902013

Print information available on the last page.

Balboa Press rev. date: 03/21/2019

Balboa.
PRESS
A DIVISION OF HAY HOUSE

To The loving memory of my Father

FOR MARLEY

Harry dug deep.

He extracted two
carrots, he cleaned them over.

He sat over the grass and put the carrots into his beak.

Those are for rabbits!

An irritating voice said.
Harry didn't take a bite.

Harry looked up and saw a cow holding a butter croissant.

May I ask who I'm talking to?

Harry said as he left.

He found a comfortable and quiet place under a tree; he sat and prepared to eat his carrots.

Those are for rabbits!

A silly voice said. Harry didn't take a bite.

Harry looked up and saw a
sheep holding a melting ice-cream.

Harry said as he left.

He found a comfortable and silence place over a rock; he sat and prepared to put the carrots into his mouth.

Those are for rabbits!

An annoying voice said. Harry didn't take a bite yet.

Harry looked up and saw a donkey holding an oily burrito.

May I ask who I'm talking to?

"Ooopsie!"

Harry said as he left.

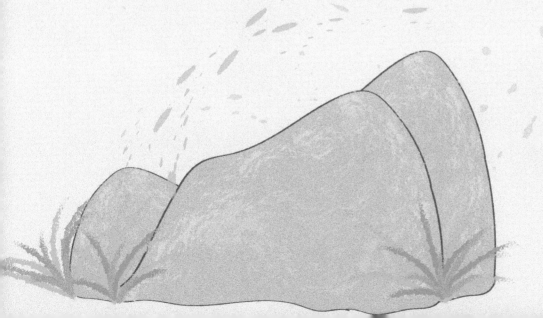

He went home and cooked a delicious cake.

He took the cake and went out.

Harry found Charlotte, Barbraaa, and Carlos.

What's that???

Carlos threw his burrito to the ground and gulped a piece of cake.

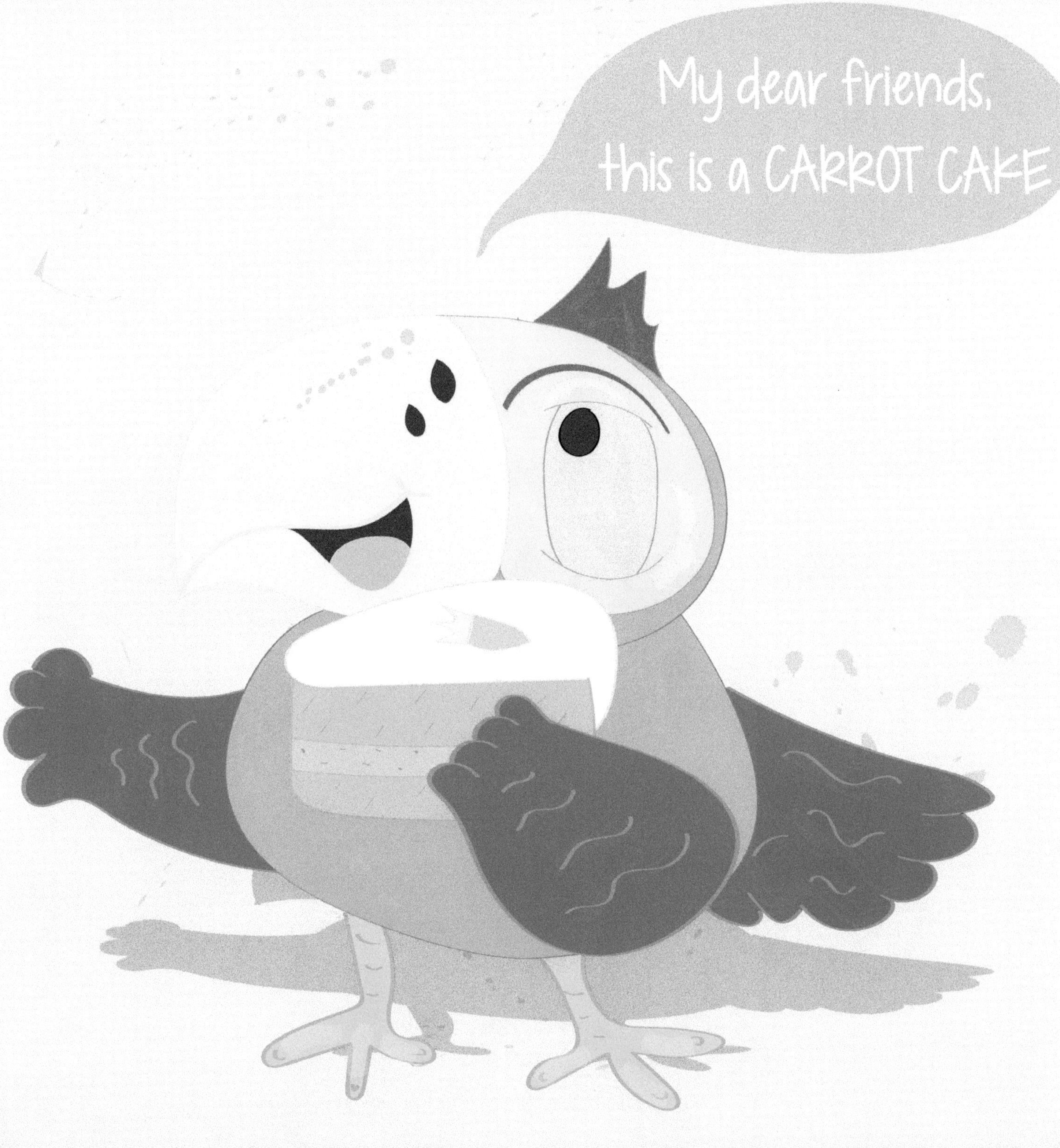
My dear friends,
this is a CARROT CAKE

THE END.

BY MARLEY

Just like Harry THE PARROT, Merri always fought with other's approvals.

One day she decided the only approval she needed was herself's, so she follows

her instincts and started to do the things that she truly loves, like write and

illustrate to name a few. She lives in the sunny and multicultural Miami with

her fabulous family of four: Hugo, Marley, Roni the doggie, and her cat AKA

gata con botas. They always have the fridge full of carrots.

CPSIA information can be obtained
at www.ICGtesting.com
Printed in the USA
BVHW021059260319
543725BV00024B/1046/P